April Foolishness

by
Teresa Bateman

illustrated by
Nadine Bernard Westcott

Albert Whitman & Company, Chicago, Illinois

Library of Congress Cataloging-in-Publication Data

Bateman, Teresa.
April foolishness / Teresa Bateman ; illustrations by Nadine Bernard Westcott.
p. cm.
Summary: Grandma, Grandpa, and the grandkids enjoy April Fools' Day on the farm.
ISBN 13: 978-0-8075-0404-8 (hardcover)
ISBN 13: 978-0-8075-0405-5 (paperback)
[1. April Fools' Day–Fiction. 2. Grandparents–Fiction. 3. Farm life–Fiction. 4. Stories in rhyme.] I. Westcott, Nadine Bernard, ill. II. Title.
PZ8.3.B314Ap 2004 [E]–dc22 2004000825

The design is by Carol Gildar.

For more information about Albert Whitman & Company,
visit our web site at www.albertwhitman.com.

For Suzanne, Jolyn, Shelley Ann, and Rebecca—
can't pull the wool over their eyes!—T.B.

For Oompah and Will—N.B.W.

Life on the farm keeps a gal on her toes.
That's what Grandma thought
as she flung on her clothes.

She grinned, for the grandkids had come for a stay.
And wouldn't you know it—they'd picked the right day!

"Grandpa, oh, Grandpa!
The cows have got loose—
I think Big Brown Bessie
just stepped on a goose!"

"Imagine," said Grandpa.
"Good gracious. Alas!"
Then he poured some milk
in a tall frosty glass.

They're squawking and
squabbling and racing about!"

"Imagine," said Grandpa. "Amazing. Oh, my!" as he popped some eggs into the skillet to fry.

"Grandpa, oh, Grandpa!
The pigs broke the gate!

They're in the tomatoes!
Oh, hurry—don't wait!"

"Imagine," said Grandpa.
"I'm really quite shaken."
He reached in the fridge,
and he got out the bacon.

"Grandpa, oh, Grandpa! The goats are all freed!

They're running around in a *smelly stampede!*"

"Imagine," said Grandpa.
"It's really quite scary."
Then he sliced the goat cheese
that he bought from the dairy.

"Grandpa, oh, Grandpa!
The sheep are all gone!

I heard that they're munching on somebody's lawn!"

"Imagine," said Grandpa.
"I hope things get better!"
He opened the closet
and got out a sweater.

"Grandpa! Oh, why won't you listen to me?
The farm's going nuts. If you'd look, you would see!"

But Grandpa just grinned as he took out the bread
and he popped in some toast for his breakfast, instead.

Then Grandma appeared. "What a hullabaloo!
Who's causing this noise—the grandkids, or you?"

"It's nothing," said Grandpa, "Ignore them, I say.
They're trying to trick me.
It's April Fools' Day!"

"But honey," said Grandma, "you'll find, to your sorrow, it's not April Fools' Day today, but tomorrow!"

Then Grandpa turned red,
and he gave out a roar.
He sped through the kitchen
and dashed out the door!

Grandma just smiled
as she pulled up a stool.
She nibbled his toast and she called,

"April Fool!"